BRIDGET FIDGET

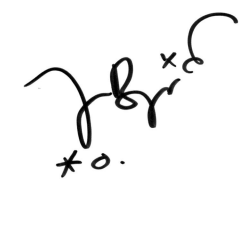

Joe Berger

PUFFIN

For Charlotte, Matilda, Beatrice and Martha – J.B.

PUFFIN BOOKS

Published by the Penguin Group: London, New York, Australia, Canada, India, Ireland, New Zealand and South Africa

Penguin Books Ltd, Registered Offices: 80 Strand, London WC2R 0RL, England

puffinbooks.com

First published 2008

1 3 5 7 9 10 8 6 4 2

Text and illustrations copyright © Joe Berger, 2008

The moral right of the author / illustrator has been asserted

Printed in China

Hardback ISBN: 978-0-141-38420-7   Paperback ISBN: 978-0-141-50100-2

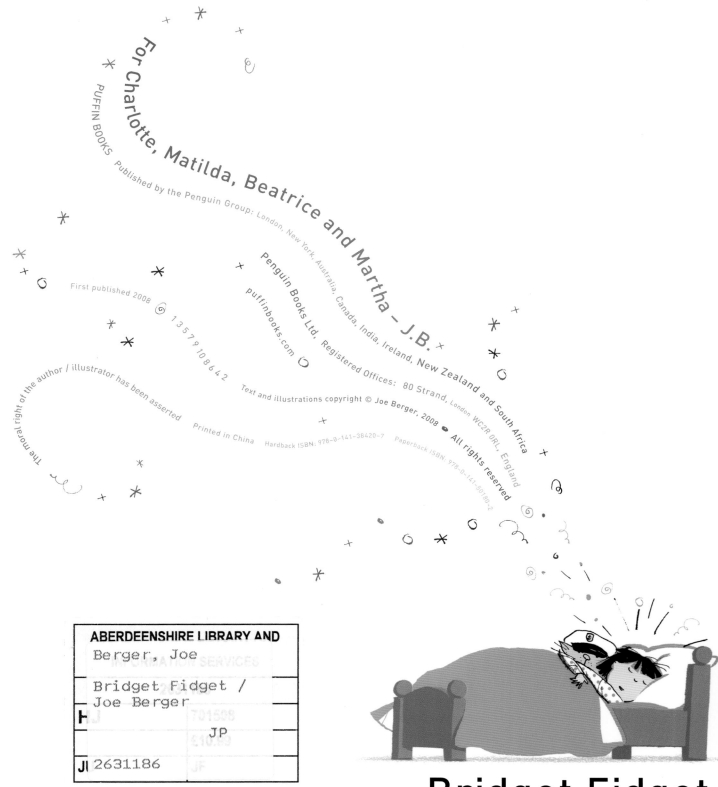

Bridget Fidget

was dreaming about pets . . . when the doorbell rang.

She **leapt** out of bed,

put her clothes on
and *raced* downstairs
with Captain Cat.

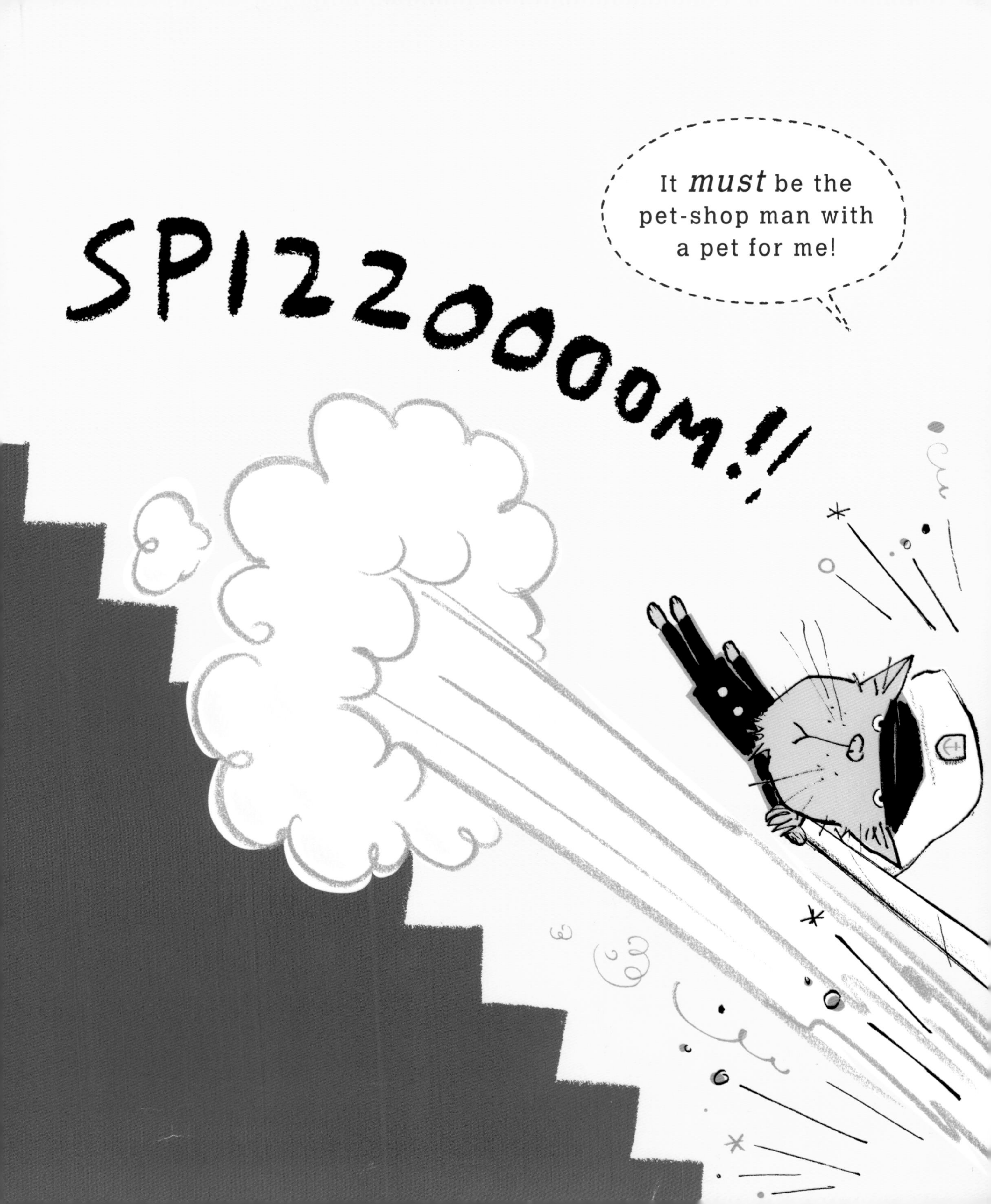
SPIZZOOOOOM!!
It *must* be the pet-shop man with a pet for me!

But when Bridget got downstairs,
all she found was a **great big box.**

FRAGILE DO NOT D

CAUTION

NOT DROP

CAUTION

HANDLE WITH CARE

It was decorated with lovely ribbons
that probably said "*Congratulations!*"
and "*Here's your new pet!*"
or something like that.

It's a bit small
for a unicorn.

This box wouldn't open.
Bridget sniffed it.
It didn't **smell**.

Bridget **shook** it.
It didn't squeak.

Bridget *rolled* it.
It didn't skitter.

Maybe it's
NOT a mouse.

Just then, the box began to make a noise.

!

It's asleep, Captain Cat! There's a sleepy little secret pet in the box and we need to WAKE IT UP!

A shower is good for waking up.

But Daddy was already
in the shower.

So Bridget tucked the box up in bed with Mummy.

Daddy didn't like the snow one bit.

He made a **LOT** of noise,
which woke up Mummy.

Luckily, Daddy cheered up
when he saw the box.

CUCKOO!

Bridget couldn't help feeling *a little* disappointed.

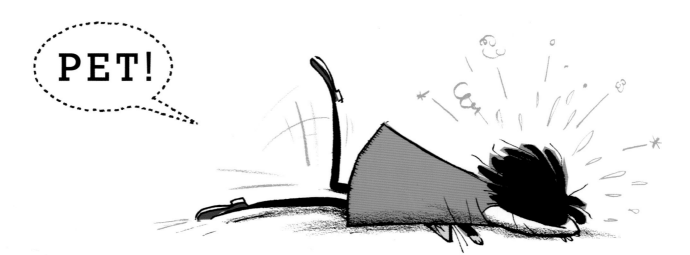

NNNNNNNNN But then, the noise started again.

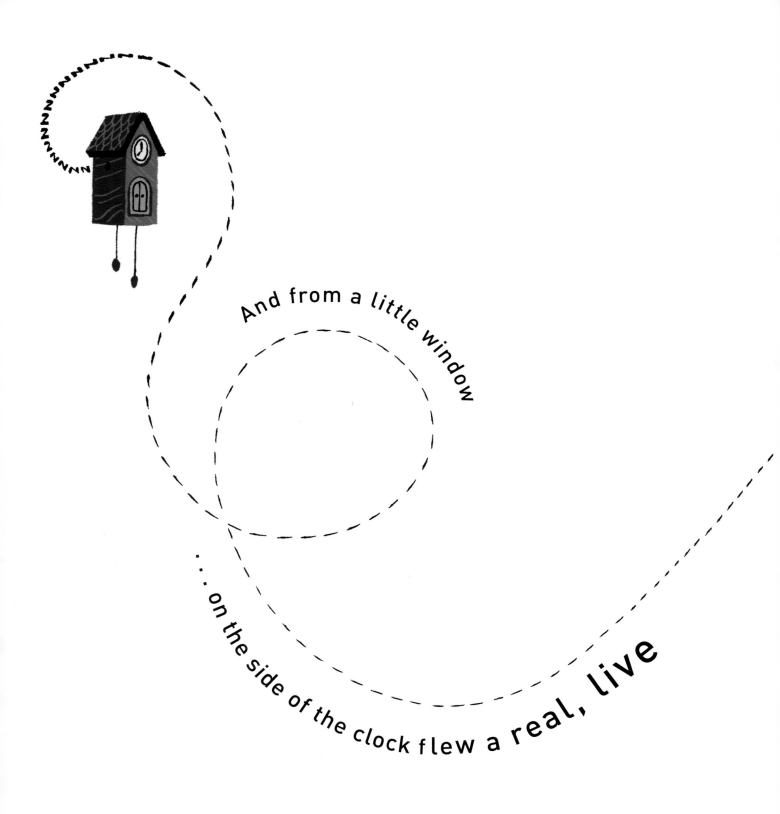

And from a little window . . . on the side of the clock flew a real, live

A ladybird that was much less **skittery** than a pet mouse

and could fly much **higher** than a pet penguin!

And as for its dancing . . .

Easily as good as a pet unicorn!

Bridget called her ladybird **Thunderhooves**

. . . the best little surprise pet in the world!